9-01 Compensatory ED

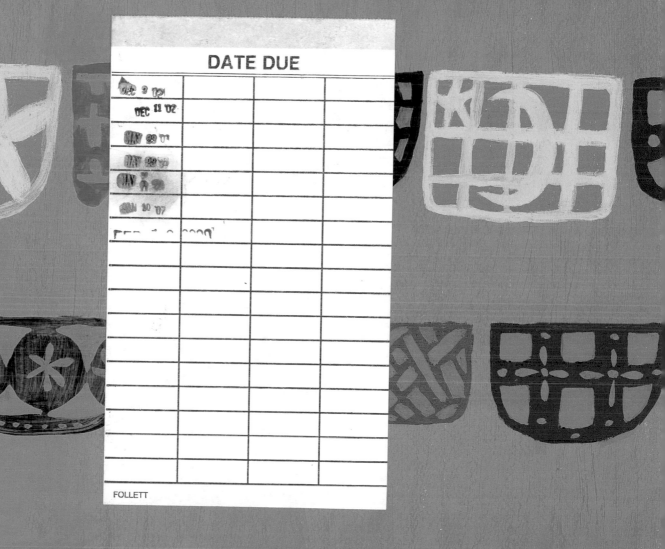

DATE DUE

DEC 3 '01			
DEC 11 '02			
JAN 23 '07			
JAN 23 '07			
JAN 7 '07			
JAN 30 '07			
FEB 1 3 2009			

FOLLETT

For my parents, Joseph and Jeannine Rehling, who encouraged me to dream,
and who instilled in me the belief that anything dreamed can be achieved.

I would like to thank my family, especially my husband, Byron, my children,
Lorien and Nicholas, and my sisters, Julie and Lynn, for their love, support, encouragement,
and patience. Credit for this book's existence must also be given to my good friend,
Andrea Shears, who has given me her time, her ear, gallons of coffee, and occasionally
a much needed shove. Finally, I would like to thank my editor, Amy Novesky,
and her colleagues at Chronicle Books. – K.R.E.

For my mother, who read me stories from Greek mythology when I was little,
and who kindled my love for pictures and stories; for my sister, Margaret, for her love and
support; for my brother, George, who is so special to me; and for Elizabeth O., who is such
a good friend. Also for my cat, Cowboy, who loves me even when I am in a bad mood.
– C.B.C.

Text ©1999 by Kristyn Rehling Estes.
Illustrations ©1999 by Claire B. Cotts.

Art direction by Madeleine Budnick and Carrie Leeb.
Book design by Carrie Leeb, Leeb & Sons. Typeset in Bernhard and Linoscript.
The illustrations in this book were rendered in acrylic. Printed in Hong Kong.

Library of Congress Cataloging-in-Publication Data

Estes, Kristyn Rehling
Manuela's Gift / by Kristyn Rehling Estes ; illustrated by Claire B. Cotts.
p. cm.
Summary: Manuela wants a new dress for her birthday, but times are hard,
and she is disappointed when she receives a hand-me-down instead.
ISBN 0-8118-2085-8
[1. Birthdays-Fiction. 2. Gifts-Fiction. 3. Family life-Mexico-Fiction. 4. Piñatas-Fiction.
5. Mexico-Fiction.] I. Cotts, Claire B., ill. II. Title.
PZ7.E7494Pi 1999
[E]-dc21   98-39605
                                CIP
                                AC

Distributed in Canada by Raincoast Books, 8680 Cambie Street, Vancouver, British Columbia V6P 6M9

10 9 8 7 6 5 4 3 2 1

Chronicle Books, 85 Second Street, San Francisco, California 94105

www.chroniclebooks.com

Manuela's Gift

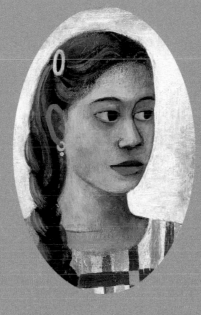

by Kristyn Rehling Estes

illustrated by Claire B. Cotts

chronicle books · san francisco

Manuela opened her eyes. She had been dreaming of a yellow party dress the color of the rising sun. For a moment she wanted to burrow back into her pillow, but the morning air brought the scent of warm bread to her nose, the murmur of voices to her ears. Manuela suddenly remembered what day it was.

Just last week Mama and Abuela had asked, "What do you want for your birthday, Manuela?"

"A new party dress," she had replied.

Manuela also wanted a pair of cream-colored boots like her friend Lupe's. She hadn't dared wish for both. But this was her birthday and anything could happen.

Mama was warming tortillas at the
stove. With quick hands she lay the white
dough against the blue flame. Abuela sat
shelling beans at the worn table, her feet
propped up on a little stool.

"Good morning, Mama." Manuela sat down next to her grandmother. "Good morning, Abuela." She carefully took a work-weary foot in her hands and began to rub.

"I was counting the moments until you woke up," Abuela said with a smile.

Manuela, Mama, and Abuela worked in the early morning quiet until the screen door slammed and Papa came inside.

"Is that my girl?" he asked. "I think you grew in the night. You're too big to be my Manuela."

"It's me, Papa." Laughing, Manuela ran to him, and he bent down to take her in his arms. The scent of him was clean and rich, like the earth in the fields, and his mustache tickled her cheek.

Papa nodded to Mama, and she left the kitchen and returned holding something behind her back.

"Happy birthday, Manuela." Mama's face was glowing as she held the dress before her.

Manuela knew the blue fabric at once. It was one of Mama's dresses, only it had been cut to fit Manuela. Surrounded by her family's smiles, she could feel a strange heat in her cheeks.

"It's beautiful," she managed to say. Her fingers touched the familiar fabric.

"You'll be the prettiest girl at the party," said Mama. "Don't forget to save a dance for me," laughed Papa. "She'll be strutting like a rooster if you don't stop," teased Abuela.

"All right," said Mama, "there's work to do."

Mama left the kitchen to put away the gift. When she came back, she stopped for a moment and looked hard at Manuela's flushed face. Manuela saw only the floor at her feet.

Mama handed her the scrap bowl. "Take this out to the chickens, and I'll have something for you to eat when you come back." Manuela took the bowl and turned to go. Mama's dark eyes followed her.

She forgot all about feeding the chickens.

In the still coolness of the barn Manuela threw herself on the hay. There would be no new yellow party dress. No boots like her friend Lupe's.

A dry breeze stirred the hay where Manuela lay, and a splash of color caught her eye. The piñata was shaped like a burro and was all the colors of a rainbow. It spun on a rope where it had been hung for Manuela's birthday party. Before the party, Papa would lower the piñata and fill it with sweets. But until then Abuela had told her to fill it with daydreams.

Manuela dreamed the piñata was filled with sweet candies and pretty hair ribbons, new boots and party dresses. And new earrings for Mama. A good hat for Papa.

"The chickens aren't laying much now," Mama had said in the kitchen as she flipped tortillas on the stove.

Manuela dreamed the piñata broke open and baby chicks and eggs fell softly to the ground. Mama gathered the eggs in her apron and clucked to the chicks. Manuela placed a smooth brown egg into Mama's callused hands.

"There'll have to be rain before long," Papa had said as he walked the long rows of corn.

Manuela dreamed the piñata broke open with a crash like thunder. Silver streams sparkled and fat raindrops splashed to the ground. The corn began to whisper and writhe and green and grow until its long fingers tickled the sky. Papa threw his hat into a puddle and Mama and Manuela danced in circles around it.

"These old feet are worn from the wear," Abuela had sighed as Manuela rubbed them, pushing harder with her thumbs in all the best places.

Manuela dreamed the piñata broke open and a horse plunged to the ground on four strong legs. Abuela clapped her hands with joy and jumped easily onto its back.

Manuela dreamed the piñata was filled with all the things she wanted and all the things her family needed.

And then she thought of the blue dress she had been given. Mama had always looked so pretty in it. She and Abuela must have worked long into the night—long after Manuela was asleep—cutting and stitching to make the birthday gift.

Mama came into the barn and lay beside Manuela.

"You're my favorite girl," said Mama.
"You're my favorite mama," said Manuela.
"Are times hard, Mama?"
"Times are what they are, Manuela, and all
times pass."
"I wish this time was not so hard."
"I wish my girl wouldn't grow so fast."
Mama smoothed the hair from Manuela's face. "But
grow you will, whether it rains or not, whether there are
eggs or not. We have much to celebrate."

Manuela took hold of Mama's hand—the hand that
had sewn a birthday wish into her new dress.

"Thank you, Mama."
"You're welcome, my girl."

Manuela smiled and imagined herself in her new
blue dress, dancing at her party.